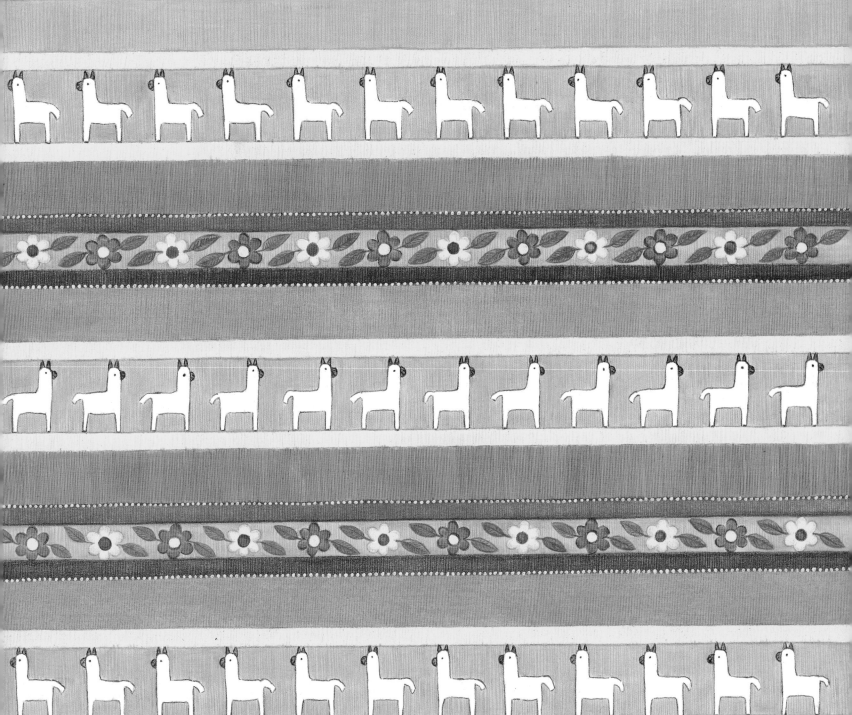

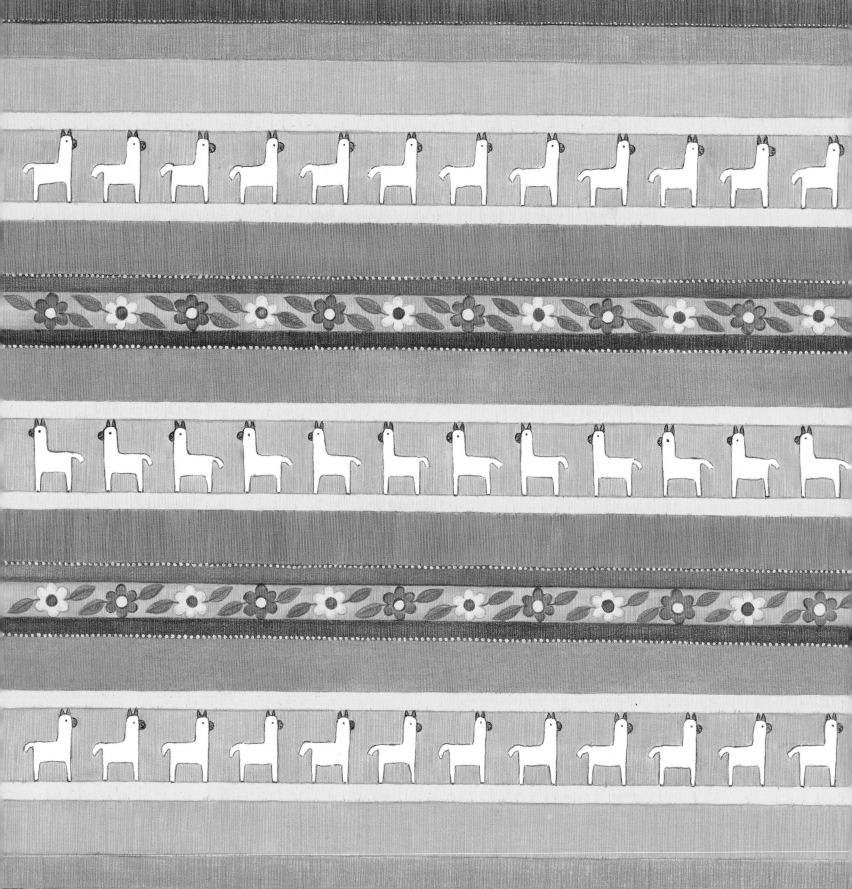

Macca the Alpaca

MATT COSGROVE

Scholastic Press • New York

For my mum, Nancy. Thank you for EVERYTHING — M.C.

Library of Congress Cataloging-in-Publication Data available

ISBN 978-1-338-60282-1

10 9 8 7 6 5 4 3 2 1   20 21 22 23 24

Printed in Malaysia   108
This edition first printing, February 2020

The type was set in Mr Dodo featuring Festivo LC.

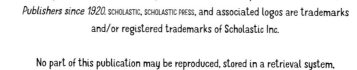

This guy is called **Macca.**

He's an alpaca!

He loves **splashing** in puddles and gives

the **best** cuddles!

Macca's days were carefree, filled with **giggles** and **glee,**

until... **DRAMA!**

A **llama.**

Harmer was mean,

quite the **worst** you have seen!

He took Macca's stuff and played very **rough.**

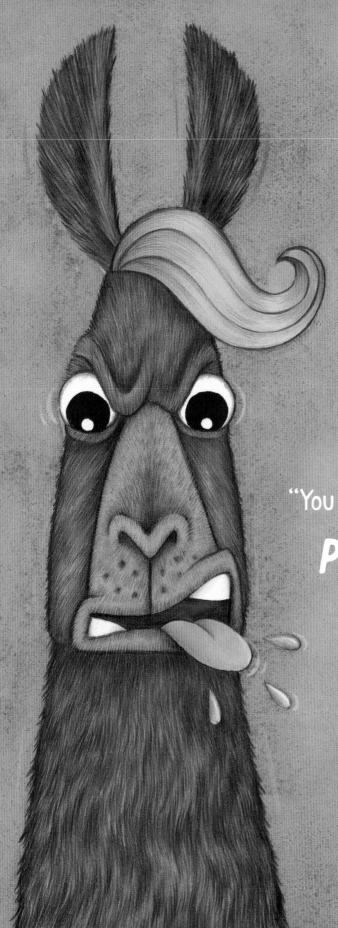

"You **PUNY** *pipsqueak,*

I'm **STRONG** and you're *weak!*"

Macca said,

"No, you're wrong,
I'm **surprisingly**
strong."

The pair made a bet and
a **challenge was set.**

"I'll move this boulder!"

Harmer pushed with his shoulder.

He **huffed, puffed,** and **nudged** 'til it finally budged.

When Macca's turn came,
he just **used his brain.**

"Easily done,
using this."

Harmer
let out a
hiss.

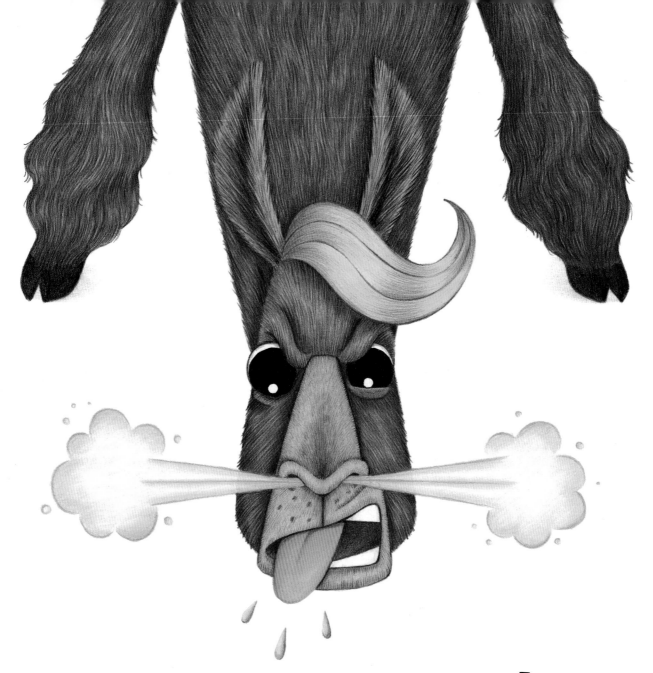

Now that llama was FUMING!

His nasty mind *zooming.*

"Okay, let's have a **race!**
Try and keep pace.
First to the top is the best . . .

full stop."

They took off in a flash
and began their **mad dash**
up the steep mountainside.

But then ...

the rocks
started to

slide.

Being **nimble** and **light**,
Macca made it all right.
As he leapt to the summit,
he saw Harmer

PLUMMET!

Some might call it karma,
as that bully of a llama

went ...

CRASH,

BANG,

and

SPLAT!

And that, my friends,
was that.

Harmer said, plainly **shaken,**

"Turns out I was mistaken,
for you've proved it quite clearly,
size doesn't matter, really."

Macca went up to the thug
and gave him

a **great,**
big...

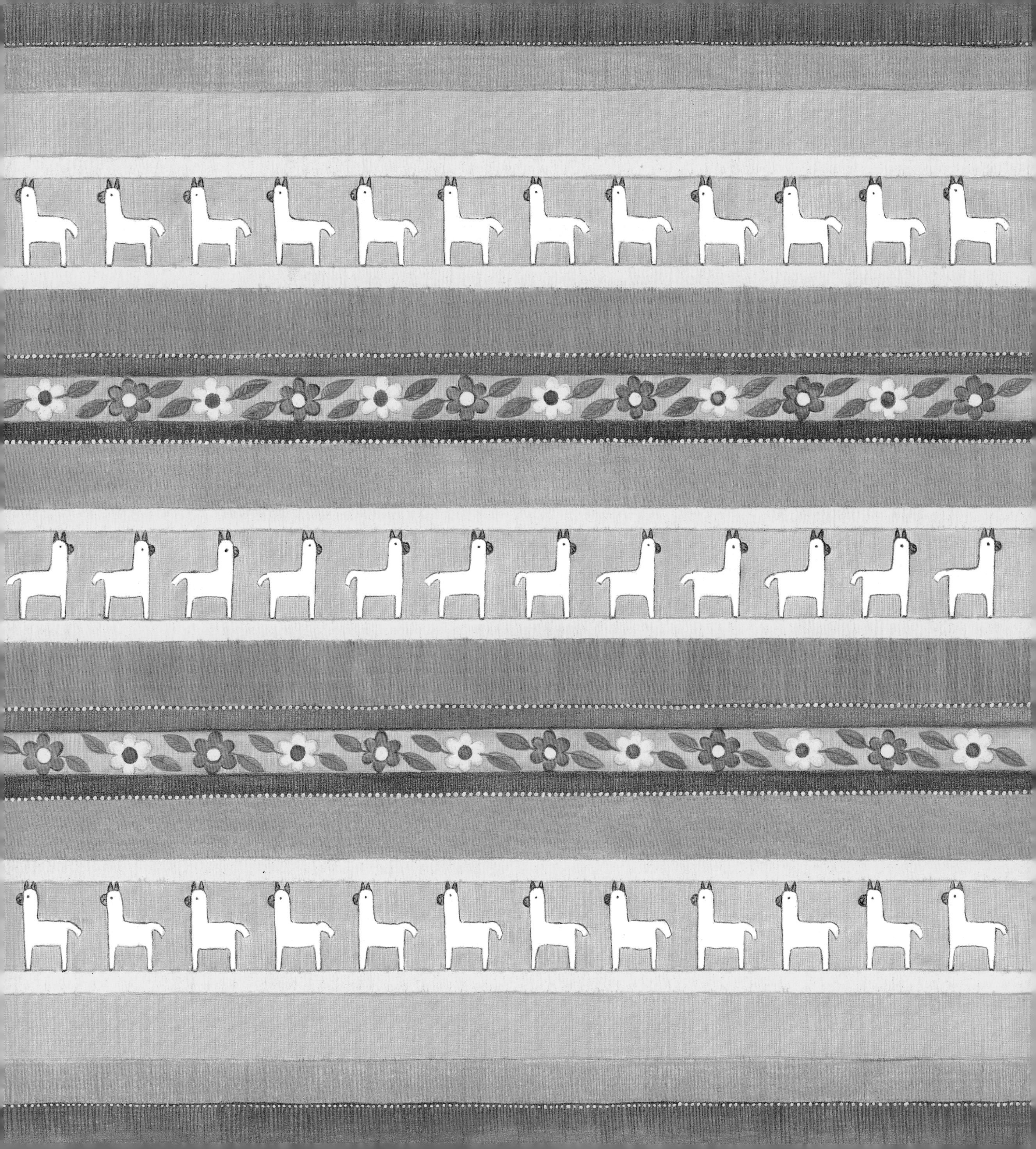

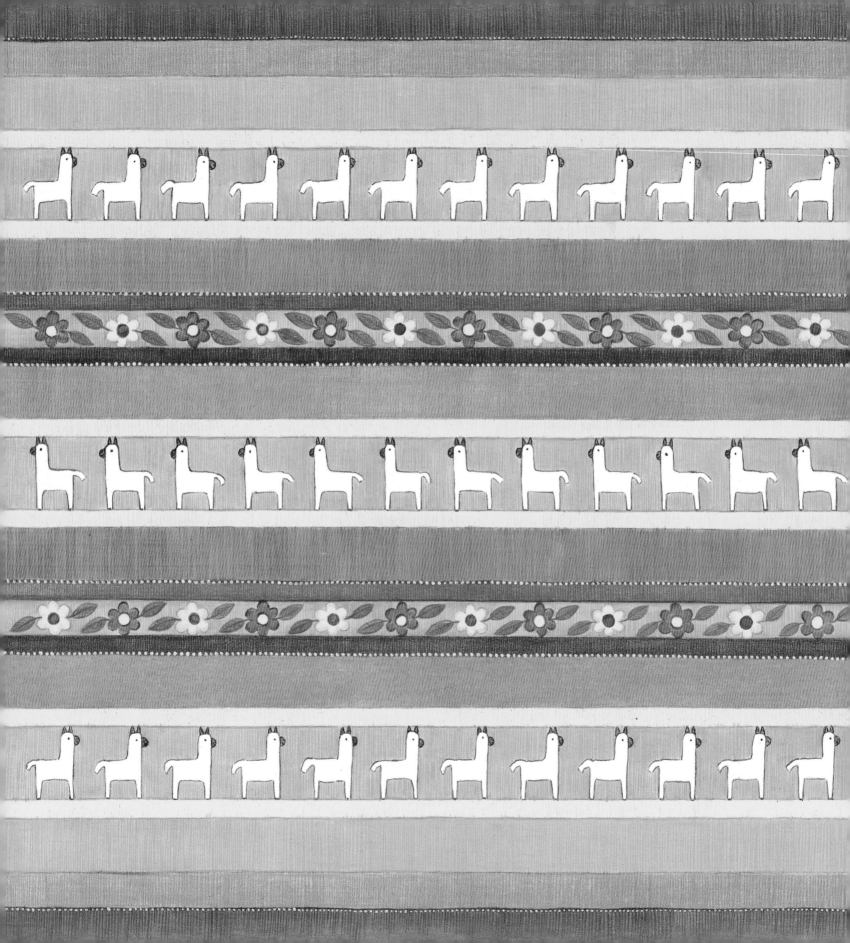